FEELING HER

A LESBIAN ROMANCE

GRACE PARKES

ACKNOWLEDGMENTS

I want to say a special thank you to my cousin, Lisa.

Her support has helped me a lot!

Lots of love, Grace x

1

"Could you rub a little harder, please?" Abbie whimpered as she tried to let go of her mind and relax her body.

"Sure, how does this feel?" Ren replied as she adjusted her hands over Abbie's right shoulder.

"Perfect. I'm sure I have done something to my shoulder. It's maybe from falling off of my bike last week," Abbie laughed as she relaxed her body onto the massage table, her wavy hair draping down over one side.

"Oh no! What happened?" Ren enquired, trying not to smirk even though Abbie was face down on the bed and couldn't see her expression.

"I took my friend's daughter out for a bike ride and ended up getting chased by a small dog. It spooked me, and I fell off of my bike, landing on the curb."

"Ouch!" Ren couldn't help but laugh slightly at the thought of a tiny dog chasing Abbie down the street.

"You think it's funny? You wait until you get chased by a dog," Abbie grinned, appreciating Ren's sense of humor.

Ren's health and beauty clinic was situated on the peaceful grounds of her home. An old, white cottage surrounded by trees, tucked away in the countryside. Ren built her clinic at the end of the garden before opening her doors for massage and beauty treatments. She always set the ambiance with lavender-scented candles, various reed diffusers, and relaxing background music. Abbie had been going to Ren for the last few months, hoping to invest more time into her mind and body instead of going out drinking every weekend with her friends.

"So, how does it feel now?" Ren asked as her hands pressed deeper into Abbie's skin, massaging the muscle below.

"Slightly painful but in a good way," Abbie exhaled, enjoying every movement.

Ren smiled to herself as she took great pride in her work. After spending years in the police force, Ren found the stress too much to handle, forcing her to leave and start over. She opted for a more relaxing career, although constant massaging was tough on the arms and back. Still, Ren loved helping people rather than fighting against them.

"I am so pleased that it's helping you. I have to say, your shoulder feels pretty tight today, even for you!"

"Hence why I booked in a little sooner. You're the best!" Abbie said with a slight moan of pain as Ren pushed harder.

Abbie worked in an office, and it was becoming clear to her that sitting down every day wasn't doing much good for her posture. After work, she would make the commute home and walk into a messy house caused by her rather selfish boyfriend, Adam. She wasn't happy, but she didn't have the energy to leave.

"Glad you think so. Have you not trained Adam yet?" Ren asked. She knew a lot about Abbie's life. They got on quite well and often chatted during the treatments.

"Ha, next joke. He can barely look after himself, let alone me," Abbie sighed.

"Oh, Abbie. This has been going on for some time. I know I'm just your massage therapist, but I also see things from an outside perspective. You deserve better," Ren replied, still kneading Abbie's flesh like dough.

Abbie smiled, her face still in the hole of the massage bed. It was nice that someone thought she deserved more because, after so much of the same shit, it was easy to forget. "Thanks, Ren."

"No worries. Anyway, I'm done on the tight part, so now, you relax and enjoy the cool down. You need to relax," Ren said as she turned the tranquil music up and dimmed the lights a little more in her bohemian-style massage room.

Her hands drifted around Abbie's back,

working her way around the shoulders, down the arms, and back up to the nape of her neck. Her hands moved down, massaging the oil in circular motions into Abbie's soft skin. Ren loved massage therapy. She loved making people feel good.

"Ah, that feels amazing," Abbie exhaled as Ren's hands moved down toward the back of her thighs, working down in circular motions to her feet. Ren liked the massage to end gradually, avoiding the abrupt end that some therapists offered.

She gradually slowed her motions, drawing the massage to an end. "All done. You take your time getting dressed, and I'll just be out the front with some water for you."

Abbie mumbled something into the fabric as she laid peacefully in the dimly lit room, surrounded by delicious scents. She took her time getting off of the bed, preparing for the reality of her life. Preparing to go back home and make dinner for her good-for-nothing boyfriend, who liked to sit on his ass playing video games all day. It used to be good, maybe for the first two years, but then complacency started to slip in, and Adam stopped making any kind of effort.

As Abbie left the treatment room, Ren was standing behind the reception counter with a tall glass of iced lemon water and a warm smile on her face. Her curly red hair was tied back perfectly into a bun, with subtle eye makeup that brought out her beaming blue eyes.

"Thanks so much, Ren. You always make my week. Same time next week okay for you?" Abbie asked as she handed over the cash.

"Of course, already booked you in," Ren replied as she passed over the glass of water to Abbie.

"Fabulous. I'll see you soon then!" Abbie quickly finished the water, grabbed her coat, and made her way out toward her car.

"Bye, for now," Ren said, still smiling as she waved her away.

Ren turned off the lights as Abbie was her last appointment of the day. Now she would walk across the garden to her cozy cottage, take a hot shower, and have her own time to relax. Her only company was her dog, Bella, but she quite liked it that way. Dogs didn't create much drama, well, at least not as much as women. Ren's past turbulent relationships had created little desire and hope for trusting another woman again.

2

"Seriously, Adam? You can't do just one load of laundry a week?" Abbie exhaled as her peaceful state of mind was ruined the moment she walked into her house. It was already eight at night, and before long, she would be in the shower and going to sleep to get up early for work again. Instead, she studied the housework, which, yet again, hadn't been done.

"Oh, sorry, babe. I got a new game today that Pete loaned me. I've been a bit busy, but it is my day off!" Adam replied, still staring at the television screen.

"So, this receipt for *Warzone 2056* totaling a whopping eighty dollars has nothing to do with it?" Abbie questioned.

"Don't start on at me about money. You're the one who spends forty dollars a week on a massage," Adam snapped, still not making eye contact.

"I'm not starting, but you're the one who moans about money all the time because you're in debt. Just don't lie to me. Yes, I spend money on a massage, but I'm not in debt, and I never have been. I'm a grown-ass woman in my thirties looking after my mind and body. You should try it sometime!"

"Blah blah blah. You come home, and it starts. Why can't we just talk like adults?" Adam replied, *still* staring at his game.

"Adam. You're not even looking at me. I asked you to help me with the housework by simply putting some clothes into the washing machine. Yet, it still looks like a dump! I can't deal with this. I'm going to bed," Abbie snapped as she stomped upstairs, trying to let go of her anger. Adam gave no response.

As Abbie undressed to get in the shower, she noticed a patch of wetness in her panties. *Jeez, what's going on?* Abbie thought to herself as she realized just how soaked she was, and it certainly wasn't from a messy house or a lazy boyfriend fetish. *Abbie, what's going on? This happened last time too.* Abbie questioned as the same wetness had occurred after her previous massage with Ren—and the week before that, and maybe even the week before that.

She had no time to process it. Instead, she threw her clothes into the laundry basket, jumped in the shower, and turned on the hot water. Even with the blazing temperature of the water, she couldn't quite let go of the thought of her wetness, seemingly caused by Ren's touch. She did like Ren but, surely, not like that. She hadn't ever been touched by a woman before. And she wouldn't want it either. *How do you know? You've never tried.*

Abbie's mind taunted her as she tried to wash away her confusion of sexual frustration and anger. Abbie slowly slipped her fingers between her legs to discover how excited she was. She hadn't been that wet for a long time. Her fingers slipped inside easily, lubricated by her excitement. She licked her lips as the water trickled down her back. Leaning against the wall and placing one leg on the side of the shower stall, she circled her fingers around her clit and opening, massaging herself with rising pleasure. Her fingers teased her entrance, and then she slowly pushed them in to fuck herself a little. The thought of Ren's touch flickered across her mind. *What the hell are you doing!?*

Abbie's mind moved back to the feelings that wanted to overtake her thoughts. She fucked herself a little before slipping her fingers out and rubbing circles over her clit. The motions became firmer, adding more pressure to her swollen, throbbing clit. Abbie rubbed harder, letting her mind flow in any direction it wanted. The direction took her straight to Ren. The thought of Ren's hands and her magical touch sliding into her like this. Of Ren touching her in every single place.

A wholly inappropriate and erotic massage scene played out in her mind like some kind of porn movie. Abbie started to rub more as these thoughts whirled in her mind, and she came so hard, causing her legs to shake and knock her off balance. She managed to grab the edge of the shower and regain her position as the hot water trickled upon her flesh, with the pulsating orgasm still rippling in her core. Abbie didn't question anything. She simply finished washing and slid into the bed in the spare room—as far away from Adam as possible.

∽

Ren poured herself a cup of tea after a relaxing evening of bathing and self-care. Sometimes it was easy to forget about yourself when you were busy making other people feel good all day.

"Here you go, Bella," Ren offered her faithful pooch a little biscuit. Bella gladly accepted it and gave her paw for the offering. "Good girl!"

Bella licked her lips as she nudged Ren for more attention, having made her way over to the sofa. "Come on then, let's cuddle up here!" Ren patted the empty couch space next to her as Bella jumped up and snuggled close to her side. As she settled back into the comfy, well-worn couch, her mind drifted back to Abbie. *I wonder if she's okay? That girl deserves so much more. She's such a nice girl!* Ren thought to herself while Bella rubbed her hairy chin across Ren's thigh. *Anyway, it's not your business.*

Ren shifted her thoughts by grabbing her book off of the coffee table and delving into a world of romance. Ren had a huge heart with a lot of love to give but found herself becoming more guarded as the years went by. At forty-one, Ren enjoyed her own company and her independence. She knew it would take a lot for her to open herself up again.

3

"Look, Abbie!" Leanne said as she shoved her hand across Abbie's desk to show off her shiny and sparkling engagement ring.

"Wow, that's beautiful. How did he do it?" Abbie replied, trying her best to sound interested in Leanne's love life. In reality, she really didn't give a shit about her snooty colleague, who cared more about the labels of her clothes than anything else.

"Well, he took me out for dinner at our favorite French restaurant, and then at the end of the meal, the waitress brought out a glass of *very* expensive champagne. He told me to be careful when I took the glass—I inspected it and saw the ring attached to the stem!" Leanne grinned.

"Did you have to break the glass to get it?"

"No, silly. It was just attached with a string," Leanne replied.

"Ah, how romantic!" Abbie attempted to use her most expressive tone without sounding sarcastic.

"I know, he really does love me. I know we had a little mishap with that woman he was texting, but we're over it and stronger than ever," Leanne was clearly trying to convince herself that her cheating fiancé had changed his habits.

Abbie smiled and nodded her head, knowing full well he would never change. "Aw, that's so lovely."

"So, do you reckon you and Adam will take the next step?"

"Nah, not sure that we will. I'm not really into marriage," Abbie replied as she saw the look on Leanne's face change to shock.

"Really? Not into it? Well, to each their own! Anyway, I best finish off this work,"

Leanne said as she went back toward her desk.

Abbie sighed in relief. *Marry Adam? Wow, I really can't think of much worse. I have to do something about this,* Abbie thought to herself as she finished her mid-morning coffee. Abbie knew her mind was offering her clarity. She had to do something about her relationship with Adam but trying to fix it didn't seem to be doing anything. *How do I end it? Where will he go?*

Abbie's thoughts toyed with her emotions a little, but she promised herself to stay strong. She didn't want to end up old and unhappy, wasting her time with someone she didn't even like. After turning thirty, she felt a shift in her heart. Nothing was fueling the fire for her anymore. There was no passion in her life.

I mean, for God's sake, Abbie, you masturbated after your massage session! You need to get laid, preferably with someone you're into. Abbie shook off the devil from her shoulder and continued with her day's work.

Her office was filled with a variety of people, some of whom she just didn't get along with due to their utter lack of personality. Abbie had worked in the office sector for most of her career, but this job was part of the city council, dealing with complaints and issues in the local area. It paid enough, but the office hours were sometimes tedious. Living for a Friday finish felt quite tragic after so many years had gone by.

The ruminating thoughts of marrying Adam pushed Abbie into the bold realization that she needed to make some changes —and fast! She grabbed her phone and composed a text.

Abbie: *We need to talk tonight. Are you in?*

She sent the message and awaited a response. With another day off work, Abbie knew it was most likely he would be lost in his new game. To her surprise, her phone pinged.

Adam: *I was going to go over to Carl's, but I'll wait until you get back. Everything ok, sweetie?*

Even the way Adam texted her was starting to make her cringe.

Abbie: *Okay, great. Everything is alright, we will talk later.*

She knew starting some kind of drama

over text messages was never a good call. As Abbie gazed around the office, she caught her boss flirting with Sandra from Admin again. She watched how their eyes locked as they exchanged words. You could see the chemistry between them. Chemistry which Abbie was unsure she had ever experienced.

* * *After a tedious day of listening to people complain about the most ridiculous things, Abbie unlocked the front door to her house with a chest of anxiety bubbling like a cauldron.

"Hey, honey!" Adam shouted from the living room as soon as she opened the door.

Abbie tried to hide her eye roll as she put down her bag, slipped off her shoes, and made her way through to the living room to see a bouquet of flowers and a box of luxurious chocolates on the table. "Oh, wow! What's all of this for?" Abbie said with an attempted genuine smile.

"For you! I've been a bit useless lately, I know. I thought that is maybe what you wanted to talk about," Adam gulped as he sat on the sofa like a child who was worrying about being reprimanded.

"Well, thank you. I appreciate it. You are right, though; I did want to talk about us." Abbie sat down on the chair opposite and crossed her legs before taking a deep breath in, "I just don't feel... happy."

"Oh, I don't make you happy?" Adam questioned.

"I didn't say it was just you, did I? It's just everything. It all feels—stale."

"Wow, that's really cutting," Adam replied, his eyes starting to shine with unshed tears.

"I'm sorry, but you just haven't made any effort in... years. I feel like I'm living with a teenage boy. We don't have sex, you don't even talk to me, and you're more interested in fake people in a game than your actual, real-life girlfriend. I just feel fed up with everything!" Abbie exhaled as every word that left her mouth was followed by such tremendous relief. All these things that had been swirling around in her head were finally coming out. She knew that Adam wouldn't take it well.

"Okay. I get it. You hate me," Adam snapped.

"Why are you reacting like a child? You're thirty!"

"So, what can I do to make things better?" Adam asked with his arms folded and a frown across his pale, sun-deprived face.

"Look, you're a great guy with a big heart, but I just don't know if we can save this. Can you honestly say that you've really been happy too? We've had rocky patches in the past, but I really feel like I'm living with a friend," Abbie replied.

"I guess it's felt a little distant at home. I want to have sex, but I don't feel like you want me."

"I come home, clean up your mess, make us dinner, and then go to bed. That's my life. Can you understand why I don't' feel like *tearing your clothes off*?" Abbie said as she realized she had never really felt that way about anyone, let alone Adam.

"Fair enough. I don't know what to say. I guess if you don't like me for who I am, then you don't deserve me," Adam huffed.

"Wow, okay! And you wonder why I struggle to talk to you about things?" Abbie couldn't quite believe how Adam still didn't understand that it wasn't all about him. "I tell you what, I'm going to stay away tonight, and maybe even tomorrow. I need some space. You have fun playing your game."

"No, don't go!" Adam pleaded, moving towards Abbie to grab her arm.

"Why? Are you worried you might have to clean up and make your own food? Grow up! I'm leaving," Abbie snapped as she marched upstairs to grab her bag and start packing. *Fuck this,* Abbie thought to herself. She could feel the adrenaline running through her body as her chest pounded and slight nausea rolled through her. She had to go. She had to leave and get some air. Her life had become a trap. A cycle of the same shit, day in and day out. It had to change now.

4

Abbie knew that she could always count on her friend, Miriam. She took a moment to gather her thoughts before knocking on her door.

"Come in, lovely!" Miriam welcomed her through the narrow entrance.

"I can't thank you enough. I'm sorry it's late," Abbie expressed as she took her shoes off and put down her bag.

"Don't you worry. That's what friends are for." Miriam picked up a bottle of wine and winked at Abbie.

"Excellent! You're the best," Abbie exhaled.

Abbie and Miriam had met at work

years ago and became friends almost immediately. Abbie loved Miriam's dark sense of humor and kind nature. Even though they didn't really know everything about each other, it felt like they had been friends forever. It was the kind of friendship that could always be picked up from where it had left off, no matter how much time had passed.

"Come sit and make yourself comfortable. Tell me what's going on, from the start," Miriam sprawled out across one sofa, pouring wine for both of them.

"Oh, Miriam. I don't know where to start. I guess things haven't been great with Adam and me for a while now, and I just feel like I've completely fallen out of love," Abbie sighed.

"These things happen, but you can't beat yourself up about it! What made you realize it now?"

"Well, if I tell you this, then please don't judge me or anything. I even surprised myself," Abbie said before taking a deep breath.

"Come on, you know I'm the least judgemental person in the world!" Miriam replied, taking a drink of wine while awaiting the drama.

"So, I have been going to get a massage weekly in hopes of looking after my mind and body a little more. One day, I came home from my session and ended up having... uh, thoughts... about my massage therapist. I can't get them out of my head. It made me think, I have never felt that excited about Adam, so surely something is wrong?"

"Oh, wow! Is he really fit? Your massage therapist?" Miriam scrunched up her face with excitement since she loved to gossip.

"Um, *she* is fit, yes, I would say so," Abbie blushed.

"Ah, I see," Miriam said as she broke out into a giggle.

"Why are you laughing?" Abbie asked but couldn't help herself from laughing too.

"I just wasn't expecting that. I never gotten a *gay vibe* about you, but we all have fantasies, Ab. There's nothing wrong with that!" Miriam said as she raised her glass in the air.

"And tell me, what do you know about

gay vibes?" Abbie replied as she finished her first glass with a few hurried gulps.

"Oh, Abbie! Have you ever wondered why I don't speak about men? Have you ever seen me with a boyfriend? I'm a raging lesbian!" Miriam replied as Abbie burst into laughter.

"You are funny!"

"No, Abbie, I'm not joking," Miriam said and started laughing again—it had evidently become quite contagious.

"Well, fuck! How did I not know? I know you're private with work and everything, but I had no idea. I feel so silly."

"Life gets in the way, and these questions don't always crop up, plus I don't shout it out to everyone because I have no need to. I actually have a long-distance relationship with a woman in America," Miriam grinned.

"Wow! How long have you been together? What's her name? I need photos and info. God, we haven't caught up in so long. I'm sorry it's been a while," Abbie questioned, topping up the wine.

"Her name is Priscilla. We've been together for a year now. I met her when I was on holiday in New York a year ago. Don't worry about it. As I said, life gets in the way," Miriam replied as she got out her phone to show her lock screen picture of the bodacious Priscilla.

"Woah, she is totally gorgeous. I remember you going on vacation there. I can't believe I didn't know. Am I a shit friend?"

"Nah, don't worry about it! I already told you that we all have shit going on. I had no idea what an idiot Adam has been."

"Pfft, neither did I! Now, I'm fantasizing about my massage therapist."

"Well, maybe you do have a *thing* for her. That's okay, you know. Women are spectacular. I couldn't think of anything worse than sharing my life with a grumpy man—not that they are all bad," Miriam chuckled.

"Ha, maybe I do. I feel like I've even surprised myself. I'm going back for another massage soon, and now I feel a little awkward. Maybe I should cancel? Change therapists? It feels morally wrong," Abbie panicked.

"Don't be daft. Just go with it and enjoy

yourself," Miriam comforted her as she had another drink of wine.

"You're right, I'm overthinking everything. I need to stop being so hard on myself. Also, I can't believe I've basically broken up with Adam. It's just hit me, along with the wine. I told him that I needed space, but I know what I meant was that it is over," Abbie sighed as she felt a wave of anxiety about the thought of the upcoming Adam-related drama heading her way.

"Look, it will all work out. You have to have faith. Life is too short, Abbie, and you need to enjoy it. I'm ten years older than you, so I can share some wisdom. Live your goddamn life!"

Miriam grabbed Abbie and pulled her in for a tight hug.

"Thank you, you're the best," Abbie huffed as she pulled away to wipe her eyes.

She couldn't help but notice the sense of relief that spread throughout her mind and body. This could be the start of something new and exciting. This could be the best time of her life so far. They do say that your thirties are great, right?

5

Ren ran her fingers through her hair before tying it up into a ponytail. *Forty-two today, where did the time go?* she thought to herself as she put on her stretchy yoga pants for her next appointment with Abbie.

"You be good, Bella!" Ren said to her faithful furry friend as she passed her a dog biscuit.

As she walked across to her clinic, she saw Abbie pulling up a little earlier than expected. Ren noticed how she pulled down the mirror in her car to check her face over, and Ren couldn't help but smile a little.

"Hey, Abbie! It's not like you to be ten minutes early," Ren laughed as she opened the clinic door to welcome her in.

"Ah, a lot has changed in the past week," Abbie sighed.

"Coffee?" Ren asked as she walked over to the machine, which hosted a range of delicious hot drinks.

"Mocha, please," Abbie replied as she sat down on the couch and sighed.

"No problem. So, tell me. What's been going on?" Ren enquired as she prepared the drinks.

Abbie froze for a moment, trying not to let her complexion change to beet red, "Um, well, Adam and I are finished. The other night we had an argument when I tried to talk about my feelings, and then I left because I said I needed space. Over the weekend, we met up and discussed everything, but it went terribly wrong. He said that I had ruined his life and that he hopes I burn in hell. So, we are completely over, and I feel so guilty that I'm kind of happy about it."

"Wow! Well, I am not actually that surprised. Has he moved out?" Ren passed over the drink.

"He's moved in with his best friend, so it's just me now," Abbie smiled as she took a sip of her frothy mocha, "Mmm, delicious!"

"What drama. So, you're okay with it all?"

"I do feel bad for him, but honestly, I loved him like a brother. I didn't want to ruin his life; I just couldn't ruin my own either!" Abbie shrugged.

"Fair point. Will it be difficult financially now that he has left?" Ren couldn't help but think with her business brain.

"Ha, not at all. I paid for everything, hence why he had to move out."

"Jeez, if anything then, it might be cheaper," Ren raised her eyebrows and drank some coffee. "Well, anyway, everything is ready if you want to go through. Shout at me when you're all set."

Ren's calming voice had a strange effect on Abbie. It sent a little shiver down her body, like a wave of relief and comfort. Of course, that wasn't the only feeling Ren had been giving her, but she intended to put that behind her as the massage treatments were doing her body and mind a world of good.

"Sure," Abbie said as a mix of emotions swirled through her mind.

She walked into the treatment room as usual, where she removed all of her clothing except for her burnt orange underwear. As she laid face down on the massage table, she used a towel to cover her ass and the top of her thighs. It was optional, but Abbie felt a little too exposed if she didn't. Primarily due to issues with her body. From a young age, she had dealt with low self-esteem, mainly routed from high school bullies who had no idea what impact they could have on someone's life.

"Ready!" she shouted to alert Ren.

As Ren walked in, she turned up the relaxing spa music and lit another candle. Immediately, Abbie felt a sense of relaxation. "I don't want to sound rude, but can we have little talking this session? I love our chats, but I really, *really* need to unwind," Abbie asked, always cautious of being impolite.

"Of course! You are here to relax. I am at

your service," Ren replied as she prepared her oil-based lotions for the treatment.

"Thanks, Ren," Abbie replied as she let the weight of her body sink into the massage bed.

Ren's hands slowly maneuvered their way around Abbie's body, which was noticeably more tense than usual. Ren's firm fingers manipulated the skin and muscle to lead Abbie into a deeper state of relaxation. As her hands moved up towards Abbie's neck, she noticed the goosebumps rippling across her skin.

That's new for her, Ren thought to herself as a small smile crossed her face. Abbie exhaled as she let her mind go, falling deeper into the soothing touch of Ren's hands. The massage was a full-body experience, covering her shoulders, back, legs, arms, and neck. Ren knew how Abbie liked it. Firm pressure, but not too tough on the muscle. Relaxing, yet reviving. As she worked away on Abbie's body, Ren had a new sense of enjoyment in giving her this pleasure.

Ren, stay professional, will you? Her mind shouted as her eyes admired Abbie's curvaceous physique. Little did she know, Abbie was battling with the same thought as she could feel the wetness building up in her underwear. Ren's hands continued to dance around her skin as Abbie's thoughts drifted in a completely different direction.

"How's the pressure?" Ren's voice made Abbie jump a little, reminding her she wasn't in some kind of dream.

"Mmm, perfect, thanks," Abbie replied as she exhaled.

"You do seem more tense than usual today," Ren said with a smirk.

"I know, I think it's because I've got a lot on my mind. You're doing a great job, though, as always," Abbie responded, knowing well enough it was because she was crushing on Ren harder by the minute.

"Well, that's good to know." Ren smiled and continued with the massage. "Are you happy to turn onto your back now?"

"Yep," Abbie said as Ren took the towel, holding it up for her for privacy.

Abbie looked up at Ren, making eye contact as she smiled, "So, how long have you been doing this? I've never really asked."

"About ten years. I actually used to be on the police force, but I was determined to pick a new career that wasn't going to ruin my mental health," Ren replied, her determination showing through her voice.

"Oh wow, I bet that was a hard job. I'm really pleased you've done so well here. You deserve it. I'm always so relaxed here with you. You have a way of putting people at ease," Abbie smiled as she closed her eyes.

"Aw, thanks. That's kind of you to say. Do you enjoy your job?"

"It pays the bills, and I quite like the security of it. Call me boring, but I couldn't take the risk of not having a secure income. The thought of running my own business terrifies me!" Abbie replied.

"Ah, it has its pros and cons, but it's not for everyone," Ren said as her hands worked into Abbie's thigh.

As her touch moved up her leg, Abbie let out a little moan, involuntary. Ren's eyes widened slightly as she became aware of Abbie's internal enjoyment.

"Sorry, that just felt *really* good," Abbie said as she kept her eyes shut, avoiding awkward eye contact.

"At least it didn't feel bad," Ren replied, continuing the treatment in an appropriate manner.

Abbie enjoyed the movement of Ren's hands over her body. She kept her eyes shut, avoiding any more involuntary moaning. The one thing she could sense was the build-up of sexual frustration bubbling at her core. Even just looking at Ren and her attractive smile was doing things to her inside. *What is happening to me? Maybe I am a little gay!* Abbie thought to herself as she took a deep breath and let Ren work her magic for the rest of the treatment.

∽

"We're finished for today, I'll just pop outside, and you take your time getting ready," Ren said at the end of the massage as Abbie was on the verge of having an orgasm.

"Thank you," Abbie replied as she slowly started to come back to reality.

Ren made her way to the clinic lounge area, where she poured a glass of ice water for Abbie.

As Abbie slid off of the bed, she could feel the sticky mess between her legs. *You've got to do something about this,* Abbie thought to herself as she slowly got dressed. Something had to give. She couldn't continue having these massages every week if she was feeling this confused and frustrated afterward. *Maybe I'm just confused,* she said to herself, making her way out to Ren.

"Here you go, ice-cold water," Ren said as she passed the glass over.

"Ah, perfect!" Abbie took the glass and almost drank half in one go.

"So, I just wanted to check in with you. You seem a little tense today. Are you sure everything is okay?" Ren asked while standing directly in front of Abbie, with her magical hands resting on her hips.

Abbie froze for a moment as she placed the glass down on the table, "Well, um, I have been feeling a little confused."

"Confused? What about? It's okay to talk to me if you want to," Ren replied, her warming smile inviting Abbie in.

Abbie smiled back at her and took a deep breath before leaning in and placing a kiss on Ren's cheek. Their faces stayed close together for a second until Ren put her hand around Abbie's waist, pulling her in to kiss her lips. Shockwaves of excitement drifted through Abbie's body as Ren kissed her. The kiss could have lasted seconds or hours, as Abbie was losing track of time. Ren pulled away slightly and scrunched up her face.

"I'm so sorry. This is completely inappropriate," Ren said as she distanced herself a little, her deep blue eyes drawing Abbie in.

"Oh, no, I'm sorry. I don't know what is going on with me—I'll go," Abbie replied as she left the cash on the counter, grabbed her bag, and rushed out of the door.

Ren was standing in the same spot with a look of confusion on her face. She hadn't been intimate with anyone for a while, let alone one of her clients.

6

It was no surprise to Abbie that breaking up with Adam wouldn't be a walk in the park. He had left an assortment of his belongings strewn around the house, giving him good reason to just *pop over*. Abbie decided to gather them all in one big black trash bag, which sat by the front door, ready to go. Only a few of his clothes remained upstairs in the bedroom closet.

The kiss with Ren had left Abbie feeling a whirlwind of emotions. A part of her felt elated, but a part of her felt embarrassed. Clearly, Ren freaked out on some level, and now Abbie was worried about facing the awkward situation that lay ahead of her. Her other idea was to never go back for a massage again, subsequently never having to talk to Ren and suffer that awkward encounter. The other looming confusion surrounding the situation was Abbie's sexuality in question. She'd always considered herself open-minded, but this seemed to take things to a whole new level.

Sunday night was always Abbie's least favorite. It meant that five days of work was ahead of her, and the weekend was over much too soon. Abbie sprawled across the sofa with a cup of tea and a plate of her favorite chocolate cookies—because one is never enough. As she turned on the television, her phone vibrated.

Adam, leave me be, Abbie thought to herself as she grabbed her phone out of her pants pocket. Her heart fluttered when she saw Ren's name on her screen.

Ren: *Hey, Abbie. Can we talk sometime? I feel a little awkward after what happened and would just like to talk. If you're free tomorrow, could you come over for dinner? Ren*

Abbie gulped as she typed out her reply.

Abbie: *Hey! No need to feel awkward, but yeah, sure. That sounds great. I can be there by six. Okay?*

As she hit send, she immediately started to play out situations in her mind. Would Ren come on to her again? Would she push it behind her and go forward just as friends? Would she have to cancel her massages? Her mind was hushed by Ren's fast response.

Ren: *Six sounds perfect*

Abbie grinned at her phone as she felt blood rushing to her cheeks. She couldn't figure out why she had become so intrigued by Ren. She wanted to know more about her in every kind of way. Abbie had never been with a woman intimately, other than kissing random girls on nights out in her college years. *Well, I guess what will be, will be!* Abbie thought as she headed up for bed. The house seemed quiet without Adam, but truthfully, she loved it.

∼

As five o'clock hit, Abbie was ready to bolt out of the office door to get herself ready for dinner at Ren's. Monday had never been so exciting. Her workday had been long and stressful, but the thought of seeing Ren was exciting yet also anxiety-provoking.

Should I wear a dress? No, that is too much. I think I'll go for jeans and a nice top, Abbie thought to herself, blissfully unaware of the surprise waiting for her outside of her office building. After she opened the main exit door, her jaw dropped to see Adam standing there with a bouquet of flowers in hand and a sorry, pathetic look across his stubbled face.

"Adam? What on earth are you doing here?" Abbie said in shock as she placed her hands on her hips, scrunching her face in confusion.

"What do you think? I love you, Abbie. I hate being without you. Please let me talk to you, please," Adam pleaded.

"Oh, for fuck's sake, get in the car!" Abbie replied as she opened the passenger side door for him.

Adam carefully sat down in the passenger seat, gently placing the flowers between his legs. He watched as Abbie stormed around the car to get in the driver's seat, slamming the door behind her. "So, you just turn up outside of my work and think it will fix everything? What about a phone call if you wanted to talk!" Abbie knew she was extra pissed off, as soon it would be six, and she was supposed to be seeing Ren.

"No, I just... I wanted to see you. You're my world," Adam whined.

"No, I'm not. You just miss having someone around to wipe your ass, cook, and clean for you," Abbie snapped as she turned on the engine. "How did you get here?"

"I walked from my mom's," Adam replied.

"Look, I'm sorry, Adam, but I just can't change how I feel. You deserve to be happy, but I deserve that, too, and I can't pretend to be in love with you when I'm not," Abbie said as she avoided eye contact with Adam, who was clearly welling up by the sound of his sniffling.

"Fine, you really are a heartless bitch!" Adam said as he threw the flowers at Abbie and got out of the car.

"Adam, stop. I can take you back to your mom's. Don't be like that!"

"No, I'd rather walk. Fuck you," Adam snarled as he marched off.

Abbie exhaled deeply and started to drive towards home. She felt terrible that Adam was hurting, but there had been so many attempts to fix things in their relationship, each time botched or ignored by him. Abbie knew she had done the right thing, but what she had to figure out now was what her feelings toward Ren meant.

She thought about how it could just be a silly fantasy after being in a sexless relationship for so long. Ren was the only person to actually touch her body in a long while. She thought that maybe the attraction would just pass. Her mind was quickly distracted by an unusual sound coming from her car, which seemed to be worsening by the minute. *Wow, is the world against me today? This is fucking typical!* Abbie sighed as her car began to chug away, causing her to slowly pull over and stop.

"Fuck," she huffed while reaching for her phone, which was almost out of battery,

"I better just quickly text Ren in case it dies," Abbie mumbled to herself as she quickly composed a message before her phone shut down.

Abbie: *Long story, but I've broken down near Merry Way, a few blocks from the organic market. I might be late, so shall we reschedule? So Sorry!*

Abbie exhaled and tried to calm her mind for a moment. *Right, call the auto club, get your coat on, and grab a coffee from over there,* her internal monologue was helping her make sense of the unexpected drama. Abbie sighed as she got out of the car and moved to the side of the road, fastening her coat. She then grabbed her phone and called the auto service. The one-minute hold time was enough to make her crazy with how on edge she was already feeling. As soon as that call finished, she gasped as another call came in—from Ren.

"Hey, I'm so sorry, Ren! I've just called the auto club, and now I'm going to get a coffee," Abbie said in one breath.

"Aw, no. That's so shitty! How about I come and keep you company? There's a nice little coffee shop nearby that stays open until seven," Ren replied as Abbie felt a fuzzy feeling in her stomach.

"That would be really nice, thank you. Are you sure, though?" Abbie said with a giant, beaming grin across her cold face.

"It's okay. I'll leave now! No, don't worry, I'll see you soon." Ren ended the call, and Abbie quickly grabbed her bag to check her face in the mirror. She was planning to spruce herself up for their dinner tonight, but being stuck at the side of the road in her office wear didn't give her much chance.

I guess she must be into me. What other massage therapist heads out to help their client who has broken down? Not any that I've heard of. It sounds like something out of a romantic movie, Abbie thought to herself as she waited patiently. The tow service had estimated an hour wait, so at least she would have company.

It didn't take long before Ren pulled into a parking lot across the road and started waving to Abbie. As she stepped out of the car, Abbie admired her attire. Ren was wearing a pair of black trousers and a fitted shirt. It seemed she had wanted to impress, too, or at least Abbie hoped so.

"Hey! Thanks so much for coming here. Honestly, it means so much," Abbie called as she crossed over towards Ren, "I have about forty-five minutes until the service comes, so how about that coffee?"

"Absolutely. It's not quite dinner at my place, but I guess it's something?" Ren laughed, "Come on, it's just this little place over here. I like your work outfit, by the way. It's very secretarial!"

"Oh, thank you very much," Abbie replied as she walked towards the coffee shop, feeling a little shy at Ren's compliment.

"So, good day at the office?" Ren asked, tossing her hair behind her shoulder.

"Ah, it was going well until Adam turned up outside to put on a performance," Abbie sighed.

"Oh, dear! Did you manage to sort it out?"

"I told him it wasn't going to go back to what it was before, so he stormed off!" Abbie exhaled as she approached the door to the coffee shop. Ren gently moved by her side and opened it for her. Abbie smiled in response to her chivalry.

"Ah, it's not easy. Why do you think I've been single for so long, huh? Anyway, what do you want to drink? It's my treat, so go wild!" Ren said as she gestured toward the menu.

"Why, thank you! I'll have a latte, please, with a shot of hazelnut syrup. Shall I go and sit down?"

"Great choice. Yeah, go and grab a table near the window, so we can keep an eye out for the auto club," Ren replied as she walked over to order their drinks.

Abbie walked over and took a seat by the window. Without realizing it, she had a smile stuck to her face. It was more than evident that she had a soft stop for Ren. This was new for Abbie and felt like the most exciting thing ever. She waited for Ren to come to the table while the cheery young girl made their drinks up to bring over. Even though Ren was in her early forties, she had a youthful glow to her. It was something so warming that Abbie loved.

"So, thank you for accepting my invitation. I know it's worked out a little differently, but I really just needed to talk to you. I'm so sorry that I kissed you. I took it too far, and it was completely inappropriate," Ren blurted as soon as she sat down.

"Why are you apologizing? I was the one who made a complete fool out of myself. I started it! I thought you would hate me or that I would need to find a new massage therapist!" Abbie grinned as a wave of relief floated through her.

"Oh, well, that's a good thing, I guess. Can I be honest with you? I like to be honest and communicate," Ren replied.

"Sure, you can be totally honest."

"I think you're cute, Abbie. I know you've just come out of a relationship, but I think you're a wonderful woman who deserves happiness. I've been thinking about it a lot, and if you ever kissed me again, I wouldn't freak out on you," Ren said as she reached her hand out to touch Abbie's.

"Really? Well, if we are being honest, I'm a little confused, but I have to say I think you're pretty hot," Abbie said, finding it difficult to maintain eye contact.

Ren blushed slightly as she raised her eyebrows, "Oh, thank you so much! So, maybe we are on the same page then? I have been a little confused as I had no idea you were even into women. Let alone me!"

"I had no idea either. I know I have gone through a lot lately, and I don't want to hurt anyone. I know I have to put myself first and work on what makes me happy, but please don't feel bad about what happened, okay?" Abbie said as she gladly took the drink from the café assistant. "Thank you!" she said to the young waitress.

"Okay, that really puts my mind at ease."

"My question is, should I look for another therapist?" Abbie asked.

"It's totally up to you," Ren replied as she held the warm mug in her hands.

"It feels wrong to pay you."

"How about this, when you want to, I'll give you one more massage to help you make up your mind? For free, though!" Ren grinned.

"Now, that sounds like an offer I can't refuse. I could give you one too?"

"Hold on now, I don't want to scare you away," Ren joked as she caught sight of the tow truck across the street. "Oh, look over there. The truck is here! Good timing, really. I'm not sure where this conversation is going. I feel like you might be flirting with me, though?"

Abbie blushed as she tucked her wavy hair behind her ear and smiled, "Maybe. I don't really know what I'm doing, but as long as everybody is having fun, what's the harm?"

"I'm happy with fun, Abbie. It takes a lot for me to open myself up emotionally. I won't go into it, but I've been hurt a lot in the past. I can definitely do fun. Anyway, go and let the man see to your car and come back while they fix it!"

"Okay, good idea, and fun is all I need too. Well, I don't really know what I need. I just... liked that kiss," Abbie replied as she made her way toward the tow truck parked by her car.

Ren watched her make her way outside and smiled to herself. *You've still got it, and as they say, your forties are the best. I hope the best is yet to come, literally!* Ren thought to herself as she tried to shake the filthy thoughts out of her mind.

7

After being informed that Abbie's car needed to be towed to the local garage for an appointment the next morning, Ren drove her back to her house and welcomed her inside.

"Ren, thank you so much for everything. You didn't have to do all of this!" Abbie said as she hung her coat on a hook by the door and made her way to Ren's luxurious sofa.

She caught a glimpse of herself in the mirror, noticing the tired look around her eyes, and wished she had a change of clothes.

"Listen, I care about your wellbeing and

wouldn't want to see anyone stuck out there in the cold on their own!" Ren replied. "Can I get you a drink? Wine? Coffee?"

"I'll have whatever you're having, as long as it isn't cider. It gives me terrible heartburn!"

"It's not fun getting older, is it? I'm having a glass of red wine. Is that okay for you?" Ren asked as she started to remove the cork.

"Absolutely. Your home is so cozy, and I love cottages!"

"Thank you, it needed some renovation, but I'm happy with it. I'll get the fire blazing soon," Ren replied as she tied up her thick, red hair.

"How delightful. I'll have a glass, then I best book a taxi home!" Abbie replied, admiring Ren's deep hair color and the shape of her body.

"Oh, really? I meant what I said about that massage. It wasn't a joke, plus it's quite nice to have the company," Ren said as she poured two glasses of red.

"I guess I could stay a little longer then. Only if you're sure?" Abbie said as an array of nerves and excitement swished through her body and mind.

"Of course! I wouldn't offer if I wasn't," Ren replied, handing a glass of red to Abbie.

"Okay, wonderful." Abbie took a drink of the wine but was evidently tense as her upright position gave her away.

"Are you okay? You seem a little tense."

"Sorry, I actually feel a little nervous, if I'm honest," Abbie replied, struggling to make eye contact with the charming, sexy woman who had just requested she stay a little longer. She hadn't felt like this for a woman before. She wasn't sure if she had felt this excited about anyone.

"Look, just relax. I'm your friend first and foremost. I have always felt like we have got on well in our time together in the clinic. There is no pressure here. I just enjoy talking to you," Ren said as she sat down next to Abbie.

"You're right, and you're such a lovely woman. You don't make me feel weird or pressured at all," Abbie said as she turned to look at Ren before leaning in to kiss her, almost involuntary. She was so drawn to

Ren's calm yet assertive nature, amongst everything else.

Ren grabbed Abbie's thigh as she leaned deeper into the kiss. Her plump lips captured by Abbie's sweet mouth.

"You don't seem nervous to me," Ren whispered.

Abbie smiled as she pressed in closer. She traced her tongue around Ren's mouth to taste her. Ren felt a wave of goosebumps trickling along her spine as she enjoyed the sweet smell of Abbie's perfume. Ren moved her hand, placing it gently around Abbie's neck, taking control of the kiss and pulling her in closer. "You best put down the glass of wine," Ren said, and Abbie did as she was told.

"I think you're right," Abbie whispered.

They continued to kiss, and it felt like time stood still around them. Abbie moaned as Ren grabbed her waist and pulled her tight toward her body.

"Are you sure about this?" Ren asked.

"Does it seem like I'm sure?" Abbie replied and nibbled on Ren's lip.

"I guess so," Ren whispered as her hand moved around Abbie's waist.

Abbie's body flushed with heat with the feeling of Ren wrapped around her. She kissed her deeply as their tongues danced around each other, lost in the moment. Abbie stopped, feeling a sudden wave of dizziness.

"Are you okay?" Ren questioned.

"Yeah, sorry, I think the wine has hit me already, or maybe it's just the thought of you," she replied as she took off her jacket.

"It's okay if you want to slow this down. I know this is all new for you," Ren said softly as she moved her hand onto Abbie's lap.

"I have a better idea. How about you undress me and show me to your bedroom?"

"I think that's the best idea you've ever had," Ren replied and slowly stood up from the sofa. "Follow me."

Abbie walked slowly behind Ren, picking up the wine on her way. She had an edge of nervous energy ruminating through her body, but it was soon overpowered by her desire for Ren. As they entered the bedroom, Ren turned on the bedside light and lit a few candles on the dressing table.

"What a lovely room you have," Abbie smiled as she started to undress.

"Let me do that for you," Ren replied, walking over to Abbie and kissing her softly. She reached out and started to slide Abbie's trousers over her hips, followed by removing her blouse.

"I like your underwear." Ren bit down on her lip as she pointed over to the bed and ordered, "Go and lay down for me."

Abbie walked over to the bed in her black lace underwear as Ren's eyes admired her curvaceous figure. Even though she had seen Abbie's body during massage sessions, this was entirely different. This felt completely new. Abbie laid on top of Ren's sheets, parting her legs slightly and reaching to tease her clit.

"Did I say that you could touch yourself?" Ren asked. She moved closer to Abbie, kneeling on the bed by her side.

"You didn't, but I like it more when you place demands on me," Abbie moaned.

"Well, you best learn to listen. Keep your hands above your head. Let me get to know your body," Ren said as her eyes widened at the exquisite moment of discovering Abbie's desire to be submissive.

Abbie moved her hands underneath the pillow, letting her body relax as Ren's fingers met her skin again. Ren's hands then began to trace up Abbie's thighs, but this time they went higher up than any massage treatment. Circular motions of Ren's fingertips pushed into her soft skin as each movement felt so sensitive. Ren continued to move her hands up Abbie's sides, tracing around her breasts before gently grabbing them and moving her lips closer to suck on her soft pink nipple through the sheer lace of her bra. Abbie moaned as she ran her hand through Ren's hair.

"Keep your hands up there," Ren demanded and stopped touching her.

Abbie bit her lip, closed her eyes, and did as ordered. Ren smiled and moved her fingers down to trace the thin fabric of Abbie's underwear. She could feel the wetness seeping through the lace. Ren couldn't resist her. She moved her head down and bit at her panties, slowly moving them to the side. Abbie jolted with excitement as Ren pushed her tongue deep inside of her, lapping up the wetness as if it was the best thing she had ever tasted.

"Oh my god, that feels amazing," Abbie moaned as her fingertips dug into the pillow.

Ren continued to enjoy every lick as her hands moved around Abbie's thighs, squeezing and grabbing them, pulling her closer to her mouth. Ren moved her lips around Abbie's swollen clit as she brought her hand around from her legs to push her fingers slowly inside, curling them up deep inside. Abbie moaned louder as Ren began to fuck her deeper, her tongue still sucking her clit.

"I want you to bend over for me," Ren demanded.

Without hesitation, Abbie grinned and turned herself over on Ren's bed. Ren knelt behind her, removing her panties completely before slowly pushing two fingers inside Abbie's drenched core once again. With one hand around her hips, Ren could play with Abbie's clit, engorged with excitement. Ren fucked her deeply, enjoying the sound of the wetness as she plunged into her. Abbie thrust back toward her, wanting more. Ren pushed a third finger inside of Abbie, stretching her slightly as she started to rub her clit with more pressure. Her talented hands translated well as Abbie screamed, shuddering with the most blissful orgasm she had ever experienced. Ren kissed her back as she remained inside of her, enjoying the feeling of Abbie's core tensing around her fingers.

"Fuck," Abbie exhaled as her body went limp.

Ren removed herself and laid on the bed next to Abbie, fully collapsed in orgasmic pleasure. "You certainly enjoyed yourself," Ren said between heavy breaths. It had been a while since she had had sex with anyone, but Abbie definitely unleashed something within her.

"You can say that again," Abbie giggled.

"So, you surprise me," Ren replied.

"I do?"

"Yeah, I always really liked you as a person, but everything just feels so different now," Ren smiled as she moved closer to Abbie.

"So, what can I do for you? I have to be honest, I'm pretty nervous. I feel embarrassed saying it, but this is all new to me," Abbie blushed.

"What you can do is lay right there and relax. There is no rush for anything. I'm quite satisfied," Ren replied before kissing Abbie gently.

"Really? Are you sure?" Abbie asked in shock as straight sex seemed to always end when the man found his release, whether or not the woman had found hers.

"Absolutely. Like I said, I'm satisfied," Ren grinned as she reached over to the bedside table to grab their wine.

"So, how long have you been single? Giving orgasms out like that, it surprises me that you are," Abbie enquired with a smirk on her face.

"Quite a few years now. I had a string of serious relationships beginning at twenty-four, but they all ended up in tears," Ren sighed, still keeping a smile on her face.

"Oh no, what happened?"

"Well, the first one cheated on me... with my cousin's husband. The second one turned into a friendship as the connection and spark disintegrated, and my last ex was while I was working on the police force."

"What happened with the last one?" Abbie replied as she took her wine and stretched her legs out.

"I had a bad time when I was on the force—it was so stressful—and every day felt thankless. Truthfully, I stopped putting time into our relationship, and she started pulling away from me. Things were good during some points of it, but it just ended in her walking away. It hurt me pretty badly, but we were never really that compatible. I think that's just the thing. I haven't really found anyone who I feel truly connected with."

"What do you mean? What would be your ideal compatibility?" Abbie asked.

"Well, it starts with the little things like what kind of movies she enjoys and what music she likes. It's nice to share those little interests. Then it's things like where she enjoys living. Those city folks do not always enjoy the beauty of the countryside. Then I think it's about her values and what she places importance on. All of those things add up, and if you are really dissimilar, in time, it starts to show," Ren said as she finished her glass of wine.

"You are so wise," Abbie replied as she admired Ren.

"I'm almost a decade older than you, so I guess it comes with time. Anyway, enough about me, tell me more about you. I feel like I know you pretty well, but only on a surface level."

"Mmm, I don't know what to say, really. I work in a typical nine-to-five office job. My job isn't that exciting, but I enjoy the security and routine. I have worked hard to build up my career. I love my friends and what family I am close with. I love animals, being outdoors, meeting new people. I thought I loved Adam, but I was so wrong. Oh, and I love pizza!" Abbie replied as she laughed.

"Oh, yes! Pizza is the best. You know what, Abbie, I'd like to get to know you a little more. Maybe we could meet up more often but without the car drama this time."

"I think that would be perfect," Abbie replied, then couldn't help but smile.

"I have to be honest with you, though. I really think I'm looking for light-hearted fun. I feel like I have had my hopes crushed more than enough times."

"It's okay, I get it. I won't go all crazy on you!" Abbie smirked as part of her began to worry she might like Ren more than Ren liked her.

"Thank you for understanding. Anyway, how about I order a pizza?" Ren asked as she grabbed her laptop.

"Oh my god. Yes!"

8

It had been a few days since the night at Ren's, and Abbie could not stop thinking about how amazing it was. The sex, the company, the laughter. It was the best she had felt in a long time. The problem was, she couldn't help but think of Ren from the moment she woke until she fell asleep. Abbie was waiting for Ren to text, but there hadn't been any contact yet, which was driving her crazy.

Just relax, she said light-hearted fun, and this is obsessive, Abbie thought to herself as she showered away her day of work. Luckily, there had been no word from Adam, but it didn't stop her mind from dragging her back toward what Ren could be up to. Never in her life had she felt this way about a woman. She simply couldn't get enough. *Oh, fuck it! I'll text her,* Abbie thought as she grabbed her phone from the vanity as soon as she got out of the shower.

Abbie: *Hey, I was wondering if you want to get together soon? You could come to my place or we could go out somewhere?*

As Abbie sent the text, she felt a certain relief, but it was also tied to a worry that her feelings were snowballing out of control. As she laid in bed, all she could think about was how it would be so much better with Ren's hands drifting over her skin.

∼

REN HAD BEEN SUPER busy with clients. The work had really picked up, and she wasn't complaining. With little overhead, she could see her bank balance starting to build up. Doing a job that she enjoyed, which also paid well, seemed like the best gig ever. Her time on the police force was really quite traumatic as it dampened any good that she thought there was in the world.

Ren had one more late booking left for the day, a new client. As she set up the room, she heard a knock on the clinic door and went out to let her client in.

Fuck! Ren thought to herself as the woman standing behind the glass door was Phillipa Rose. Ren and Phillipa had a history. They met on a night out in a neighboring town after being introduced by a mutual friend. Ren almost fell for her instantly, but Phillipa knew how much power she possessed. Her long blonde locks of hair and emerald, green eyes drew people in without hesitation, along with her sparkling personality.

"I told you I'd come for a treatment here one day!" Phillipa grinned, flashing her Hollywood smile as she entered the clinic reception.

"Wow, I can't quite believe you're here. I thought you moved to London?" Ren replied as she grabbed two bottles of water.

"I did! I'm back now, though... obviously," Phillipa smirked as she perched on the couch. "So, how are you doing? Last time I saw you, well, we had a lot of fun!"

It wasn't often that Ren blushed, but she felt a wave of heat moving across her face. "I've been good, thank you, very good. Business is going well, and it's keeping me out of trouble."

"Oh, but trouble can be so much fun," Phillipa winked as she tied her locks up into a bun.

"Ha, I guess so. I need to fill out a new client form with you. It won't take long," Ren said as she sat down next to Phillipa.

"Look, I don't want to be rude, but how about we save all of the politeness, and you just fuck me like you did the last time I saw you?"

Ren couldn't help but fill with excitement as her core pulsated at the thought of fucking Phillipa. "Wow, you're as blunt as ever still? You know I love that."

"I like to get to the point. I need some fun around here. I need someone to make me feel amazing the way I know you can," Phillipa touched Ren's thigh, squeezing it a little.

Ren couldn't quite believe what was

happening. This felt like some kind of filthy fantasy. Phillipa Rose turning up out of the blue, all sexy and ready to be taken. How could she resist?

But what about Abbie? Ren's thoughts flickered. *Well, you told her you're only looking for fun. Nothing is exclusive,* Ren said to herself as Phillipa awaited a reply.

"So, are you going to kiss me or not?" Phillipa asked as she squeezed Ren's thigh a little more.

Ren felt her stomach flip as she leaned in with a kiss, followed by pulling her closer and undoing her top. Phillipa liked to be dominated, and Ren knew what she was doing.

"You filthy bitch. I think you should go into that room and get on the bed. I made it all nice for your massage, but we can set that aside," Ren said as her professionalism went out of the window when it came to Phillipa.

Without hesitation, Phillipa stripped and made her way into the room, where she laid face down on the massage bed, parting her legs ready for Ren.

"You don't mess around, do you?" Ren

smirked as her eyes widened upon Phillipa's presentation.

"Look, I'm here for fun, and I know you can give it to me," Phillipa said as she raised her ass up into the air.

Ren walked over to Phillipa, moving her hands over her body and caressing her tanned skin. Phillipa was always jetting off somewhere in the sun, making the most of her holiday time. Her fancy job paid well, but she was sick of the stress, which was something else that Ren could relate to. Even though the police force was never fancy. Phillipa moaned as Ren's hands moved around her body, warming up her skin.

"Turn over, I want to see your face," Ren said as she watched Phillipa turn herself around on the bed.

Ren put out her hand and pulled Phillipa up to perch her on the side of the bed. Phillipa opened her legs and wrapped them around Ren's ass, squeezing her in closer. Ren hadn't had a chance to undress, but Phillipa was much more of a receiver than anything else. Her hands lightly scratched the skin under Ren's top as she kissed her deeply, so full of want. Ren parted Phillipa's thighs with her hand and slipped her fingers in between her legs, feeling the wetness that had flooded her core so rapidly.

"You are quite excited. I love it," Ren whispered into her ear as she started to rub circles over her swollen clit. Phillipa responded only by gentle moaning, craving to be fucked.

Ren pushed her fingers inside and started to fuck Phillipa on the side of the bed. She couldn't help but briefly think about Abbie. She didn't want to hurt her, but she also made it clear she wasn't tying herself down. She needed to have some fun before another woman could hurt her again. She needed to be sure of herself and what she wanted. Right now, she couldn't deny that she was enjoying herself as she fucked Phillipa hard and deep, which was rewarded by a gush of wetness that squirted all over Ren's hand and wrist. Phillipa moaned louder as she wanted it harder and fast. Ren grabbed her hair, pulling her in to kiss her deeply as she fucked her how she needed it. Phillipa tensed around Ren's fingers before asking, "Please, can I touch my clit, pretty please. I want to rub myself for you."

Ren nodded in agreement as she continued to fuck her passionately. Phillipa's hand with its bright-colored nails moved in between her legs, her fingers moving in a circular motion against her swollen clitoris. It didn't take long before Phillipa reached the height of climax, and her legs began to spasm around Ren, her hot center tightening so much that it was hard for her to move.

"Fuck, that is just what I needed. I knew I could count on you," Phillipa moaned as she laid back onto the massage bed. Ren had to admit she enjoyed Phillipa's sexual drive and her casual attitude toward sex.

"I have to say, that was rather enjoyable," Ren replied as she went to grab some water, noticing the notification flashing on her phone.

Fuck, it's Abbie, Ren thought to herself, all of sudden aware that her actions with Phillipa might be hard to explain. *Best not explain them, as it would only hurt her feelings.* Even though Ren made her intentions clear, she knew how sensitive Abbie was, and she never wanted to hurt her feelings. Ren could detach herself emotionally when it came to casual sex. As a sexually-driven person, she could just take it for what it was.

Ren ignored the message and passed Phillipa her clothes along with some water. "Thank you very much," Phillipa grinned as she started getting dressed.

9

Abbie's day off work was filled with dread. She sat on her couch with a cup of tea as her thoughts whirled around her mind about Ren. *Why hasn't she texted me back? Has she freaked out on me?* Abbie thought as a million possibilities ran through her mind. She just could not stop thinking about her. Nobody had ever made her feel that excited before.

The miserable weather made the outside look gloomy, causing Abbie to grab her big fluffy blanket and cuddle up on the sofa. She reached out for the remote and flicked on Netflix with the hope of distracting her mind and escaping for a few hours. After a half-hour of flicking through potential movies, Abbie's heart jumped as she heard a knock on the front door. Her mind immediately conjured the image of Ren standing there with her wild red hair damp from the rain and a bunch of flowers in her hands. To her dismay, she opened the door to see Adam standing there with his mom and a few duffel bags.

"Oh, morning, you two!" Abbie said, attempting to be kind and friendly.

"Morning. I'm here to get the rest of my things. That'll be all," Adam replied.

"Lovely to see you, Abbie. I hope everything is okay with you," Adam's mom said as he threw a glare in her direction, unhappy about her being so nice to Abbie.

"Good to see you too. Can I get you a drink?" Abbie replied.

"No. We won't be long," Adam said, avoiding eye contact and barging past her.

Abbie looked at his mom as they both rolled their eyes. She clearly knew how immature he could be.

As Adam stormed off up the stairs, his mom held back and moved next to Abbie.

"I understand it's been hard for you, and I'm devasted, but you have to do what makes you happy," she whispered as she grabbed Abbie and hugged her.

"Thank you, Marion. We don't have to lose contact!" Abbie replied as she squeezed her back.

"Of course not, darling!"

"Oh, best friends now, are you?" Adam huffed as she stared from the stairs and threw down his bag of clothes.

"Stop acting like a child!" Marion chastised as she grabbed his bag and tossed it out of the front door.

"There's a bag by the door with some more of your stuff from down here," Abbie said and pointed to the black trash bag.

Adam stalked over, grabbed the bad, and stormed out without saying another word.

"Sorry about my son, Abbie. I'll call you sometime. Bye," Marion said as she followed her son out of the door.

Abbie couldn't help but smirk as she let out a sigh. She was so damn pleased that she had ended it with him.

∼

Ren had a busy morning with clients and had simply forgotten to reply to Abbie. She really liked her but was cautious of it becoming too intense too fast. *I best text her back now,* Ren thought as she finally had a break scheduled into her day.

Ren: *Hey, lovely! I'm sorry for the delay. Are you free this afternoon? Feel free to come over, and I can cook us something? Ren*

As she hit send, thoughts of filthy Phillipa scattered across her mind. She didn't know if she should tell Abbie, just to get the truth out. She couldn't but worry that Abbie might not understand the detachment of emotions and sex that she felt. Ren sighed as she grabbed her hair and tied it up in a neat bun. The heaviness of her red locks made her head too hot.

Her phone pinged, and she read the response.

Abbie: *Hey! No worries, I know you're a busy woman. I'm off today, so that works for me. I'll pop by this afternoon.*

Ren smiled as she read Abbie's text. Her personality was so warm and kind. The doorbell buzzed, signaling it was already time for her next client.

No rest for the wicked, she thought as she walked over to let in Margery—a lovely older lady who came every week for a head massage.

10

"You need to cut down on the junk food," Abbie moaned to herself as she looked in the mirror, running her hands over her lumps and bumps. She had decided to put on a nice dress and make an effort after spending most of the day in her pajamas with her hair scraped up into a wild bun. Abbie started to feel nervous about seeing Ren. She wasn't sure how it would go. A part of her worried that maybe Ren had changed her mind about things. *Maybe it's because I'm confused? She wants a woman who knows what they want. But then again, she said she just wants fun?* Abbie sighed as her internal monologue droned on in her mind. She grabbed her perfume and spritzed the floral scent over her black dress before grabbing her keys and heading to Ren's house.

As she approached the front door, she noticed an unfamiliar car in the driveway. *Mmm, maybe she's still with a client,* Abbie thought as she checked her watch. It seemed bizarre for Ren to invite her over at a time when she would still be working. After knocking on the door, the only noise she heard was the sound of Bella barking. Abbie checked the side path and made her way down the stone walkway toward Ren's clinic.

The lights were shining, and she could see Ren talking to a tall, blonde-haired beauty through the window. Abbie stopped for a moment and watched. This didn't look like a treatment. It looked like flirting. Abbie gripped her handbag tightly and waited a moment longer, watching in angst as the pretty blonde girl leaned in and planted a kiss on Ren's mouth. It surprised her how much it hurt her inside. Abbie gasped as Ren let the kiss linger. *Fuck! I know we're not exclusive, but I didn't think she was a goddamn player,* Abbie thought to herself, watching as the unknown woman opened the door to leave. Ren followed behind her, catching sight of Abbie standing there in her pretty black dress, her eyes full of sadness.

"Abbie, wait!" Ren shouted as Abbie turned away and headed back to her car.

Phillipa giggled, acting like some kind of shit-stirrer, "Don't tell me that's your girlfriend."

"Oh, piss off! You're actually not a very nice person sometimes," Ren hissed.

"Don't flatter yourself. I only come here to get what I need out of you. It's always been like that with you. You're a good fuck," Phillipa replied as she blew a kiss in Ren's direction and marched toward her car.

Ren stood in her garden, unsure of what to do next. She decided to make her way to the front of the house, hoping that Abbie was still there. Hoping that she could explain everything to her. She never wanted to hurt her like this.

Abbie sat in the driver's seat as Phillipa winked at her before speeding off down the drive. *Nasty cow!* Abbie thought as she slammed the car door and reversed away from Ren's house. She caught sight of Ren standing by the side gate, her expression awkward and sorrowful. Abbie felt a single hot tear slide down her cheek. Her eye makeup was sure to smudge now. Everything felt as if it was tumbling around her.

∼

ONCE HOME, Abbie ripped off her clothes and got into the shower, desperate to scrub away the embarrassment she felt with hot water. She cried into the water at the strange sinking feeling in her chest. She felt the water beating against her skin and let out a loud scream as her rage and sadness bounced around the bathroom walls. She imagined the neighbors calling the police or coming to check if she was okay. She turned off the shower and grabbed a towel to dry herself off.

What she needed now was comfort. First, she picked out her favorite loungewear and then went downstairs, heading straight to the freezer to find a tub of ice cream. Abbie grabbed a spoon and a fluffy blanket before curling up on the sofa, flicking on the television. *I'm such an idiot,* Abbie thought. She could not believe she had let herself get so wrapped up in someone so emotionally unavailable as Ren.

Just as she was about to take her first mouthful of the decadent chocolate fudge ice cream, there was a loud knock at the door. Abbie hesitated to answer it—however, the banging continued. So, she carefully placed her ice cream on the table and mustered up the energy to get to the door.

Her heart fluttered as she saw Ren's face in the doorway. Abbie rolled her eyes and started to close the door.

"Wait," Ren shouted as she placed her foot in the doorway to stop it from closing completely.

Abbie sighed and looked up at her. "What do you want, Ren?"

"I want to apologize. What you saw, it wasn't what you think," Ren replied.

"Do you think I'm stupid? I know we're not exclusive, but you knew I was coming round. It's just rude and hurtful."

"I'm sorry. Phillipa and I had a fling in

the past. It was just sex, nothing else. I think I freaked out a little more than I thought I would about committing to a new relationship," Ren said as her words started to sound mumbled.

"I never asked for a relationship," Abbie said, tilting her head and furrowing her brows.

"I know you didn't, but I really started to have feelings for you,"

"Really?" Abbie asked, trying not to be too soft.

"Yes, Abbie. I kept thinking about you. I just wanted more of you, but at the same time, I totally freaked myself out. I've had these feelings of anxiety, and it's made me feel overwhelmed," Ren said, her cheeks starting to flush.

"Are you okay?" Abbie asked as Ren started to look a little pale.

"No, I feel a little dizzy." Ren lost her balance and grabbed onto the door.

"Jeez, come inside. You need to sit down!" Abbie said as she grabbed Ren and helped her to the nest she had made on the sofa. "Have you eaten today?"

"No, nothing," Ren mumbled as her blood sugar had most likely started to dip.

"Let me get you something sweet. You need to look after yourself when you're busy!" Abbie ranted as she went into the kitchen and brought over a sugary soda and a banana. "Here, eat this, and I'll get some proper food sorted for you."

As Abbie watched Ren eat, she felt an overwhelming desire to take care of her. She hated to see Ren not feeling right.

"Thank you for helping me," Ren said as she started to perk up a little.

"It's okay. I'm sorry you've been feeling this anxiety. Why didn't you talk to me?"

"I'm not the best at communicating my feelings. I've been hurt too many times before," Ren said after devouring the banana.

"You silly woman! I'm a human too. I understand anxiety. I never wanted to pressure you, but I was just hurt to see you kissing another woman."

"It was a mistake. I felt terrible about it. Can you forgive me? It's made me realize that I don't want to mess around, Abbie. I want us to be exclusive," Ren said as she popped open the can.

"Jeez, talk about changing your mind. You just said you were freaking out, and now you want this?" Abbie was unsure and still annoyed, even though she couldn't help her feeling towards Ren.

"I know it sounds crazy, but I didn't even enjoy being with her. I mean, it was fun, but I don't want to be messing around. I think I found something truly special in you, and I felt so terrible feeling like I'd hurt you," Ren said as she reached over to touch Abbie's hand.

"Well, you did hurt me!" Abbie flinched back.

"And I'm sorry. I want to make things right. I want to show you I care."

"Okay. But if you ever lie or treat me disrespectfully, I'm gone. I can't waste time with someone who doesn't deserve me. The reason I want to try is that I just can't stop thinking about you either. All the damn time. I've never done anything with a woman, and now, here I am, crying over you!" Abbie said as she laughed to herself.

"That makes me happy to hear," Ren said, standing up and holding out her arms to hug Abbie, which this time was accepted.

She squeezed her tight and kissed her shoulder. Abbie felt a warm surge of tingles down her back as she enjoyed Ren's affection.

What a fucking day, Abbie thought. As she enjoyed the embrace, she nestled into Ren's neck. It seemed to make all of her frustration dissipate.

11

"How do you like your eggs?" Ren asked as she called over from her kitchen.

"Well, I do like them with a kiss, but aside from that, I'll go with scrambled, please!" Abbie replied as she couldn't help but smile to herself.

Things had been going pretty well with Ren, and it seemed to surprise both of them.

"Eggs are my specialty," Ren replied as she started to whip up a delicious breakfast.

"That's good to know!" Abbie patted the

sofa as Bella approached and waited for her command. "Come on, girl, come snuggle!"

Bella loved Abbie. She jumped up on her and licked her cheek before nestling onto her lap. She could hear Ren banging away in the kitchen. "Is everything okay in there?" Abbie called as Bella looked up at her, hoping she wasn't going to leave.

"Oh, absolutely. Breakfast is nearly served!" Ren replied.

This was the best Saturday that Abbie had had for a long time. She couldn't remember the last time someone had made her breakfast—let alone the infinite number of orgasms she had been receiving too.

"Come on!" Ren called.

The kitchen table hosted a range of breakfast goods, including fresh orange juice, croissants, fresh fruit, and a plate laid out for Abbie with perfect scrambled eggs on toast.

"Wow, what a treat!" Abbie said with a wide smile as she got comfortable on the wooden chair.

"You deserve it," Ren replied with a

smile as she poured out two glasses of orange juice.

Spending quality time together had made Ren more confident that this was the right decision. It felt like a risk moving into a relationship, but now all she felt was contentment.

"You know what? I don't think I can remember the last time I felt this happy," Abbie said as she tucked into her creamy eggs.

She often wondered about her sexuality since it was all so new to her. It was surprising how comfortable and relaxed she felt with Ren, indicating she likely was much better suited for women all along.

"I am so happy to hear that," Ren smiled as she poured out coffee and tucked into her food.

∼

AFTER THEIR BREAKFAST, Ren, Abbie, and Bella were all snuggled together on the sofa. The fire was blazing hot as the rain outside pelted the windows. Ren looked to her side and was filled with pure happiness seeing Abbie and Bella cuddled beside her.

"So, shall we have a movie day today?" Abbie asked.

"Sounds perfect to me. I could just stay this way forever. I don't want Monday to come," Ren replied.

"Well, let's make the most of the weekend. It's so nice to have no plans other than spending time with you."

"It's absolute bliss!" Ren said as she grabbed the TV remote and flicked on Netflix.

Bella licked Abbie's cheek before nestling her cold nose into her arm.

"Aw, it's so sweet how much she loves you," Ren said as she stroked Abbie too.

"I love her too," Abbie replied but held back her next words. She wished she had the confidence to say that she loved Ren without worrying about freaking her out or embarrassing herself.

"The only thing is, I'm a little bit jealous of you two canoodling like that. I was thinking now that breakfast is settled, I could take you to the bedroom." Ren said, making Abbie's core tingle.

"Absolutely. Sorry, Bella, we can cuddle later!" Abbie jumped up and started to take off her clothes as she strutted to the bedroom.

"Someone's ready," Ren smirked, watching her pace ahead.

As soon as they got into the bedroom, Ren pinned Abbie down to the bed and started to kiss her gently. Her body was so soft and covered in goosebumps. Abbie moaned as Ren's hands lavished her body. Ren ran her tongue over her body, tracing her teeth over her firm nipples. Ren's fingertips teased down Abbie's thighs before running back up them again and squeezing every part of her body. Abbie's body fell back as she parted her legs, edging towards Ren with her hips.

"Please, please, fuck me," Abbie moaned. She had figured out that Ren loved her begging.

Ren leaned in and kissed her soft lips as she pushed her fingers slowly inside of Abbie, curling them up to hit her sweet spot, just how she liked it.

"Well, you do ask so nicely," Ren said as she started to fuck her deep and slow.

Abbie's clit swelled with excitement as her body pulsated with pleasure. Her legs stretched out, leaving her exposed and wanting. Ren knelt down on the bed between Abbie's thighs, thrusting inside of her, using her other hand to play with her body. Her fingertips tweaked erect nipples and lightly scratched over her flesh. Abbie writhed in pleasure as she grabbed onto the sheets, enjoying every thrusting motion. Ren moved her head down to make contact with Abbie's clit. She started to flick her tongue over the sensitive bundle of nerves, ranging from hard pressure to gentle, caressing licks. She pushed another finger inside and began to fuck Abbie harder.

"Fuck, I'm going to cum already," Abbie moaned.

Ren attempted to slow it down to make it last longer, but it was too late. Abbie called out Ren's name as her back arched and she hit the peak of her climax. Ren bit her lip as she watched Abbie cum for her. She loved watching her cum.

"You are so fucking delicious," Ren said

Feeling Her

as she leaned in to kiss her, moving Abbie's ashy, wavy hair out of her face.

"Oh my god, I just can't contain myself," Abbie giggled as she kissed Ren. "I want to make you cum like that."

"How about I lay down here, and you can taste how wet you make me," Ren said as she laid next to Abbie and smiled.

"With pleasure," Abbie replied, kissing down Ren's body.

It wasn't long before Ren took charge and grabbed hold of Abbie's head, slowly dragging her in between her legs. Directing Abbie to her hot pulsating core, she knew this wouldn't take long.

Abbie moaned to herself as she started to lap at the wetness she had created. Ren grabbed hold of her hair and pulled her in deeper before thrusting against her face.

"You're so good to me," Ren said as she thrust harder.

Abbie started to moan with enjoyment in between pleasuring Ren with her lips and tongue. She loved the taste of her. She loved the sensation of Ren's wet excitement around her mouth. Sex had never been so enjoyable.

Ren started to feel her legs tingle as a wave of pleasure began to build. She grabbed Abbie's head and pulled her in closer. Her dominance over Abbie excited her even further, causing an explosive orgasm just as Abbie sucked her clit, lightly nipping at the tight bud. Ren gushed slightly onto her face, without even realizing she was making a mess of Abbie and the sheets.

"Oops, sorry about that!" Ren giggled in between heavy breaths as her body continued to spasm.

"Please, do not apologize," Abbie replied as she licked her lips and climbed her way back up to lie next to Ren. She relished the sticky wetness still covering her face—the sweet smell of Ren's sex.

"You're fucking wonderful," Ren said, kissing her deeply and tasting herself on Abbie's lips and tongue.

"I could eat you all day," Abbie panted.

"Only if you're allowed," Ren raised her eyebrows and smiled softly.

The dynamics were perfect.

"Do you remember when we spoke about finding compatibility with someone?" Ren asked, turning on her side and grabbing the duvet to cover them both.

"Yes?"

"Well, Abbie, I think I've found what I was looking for. I feel like I've been waiting for you all along," Ren spoke softly as she stroked Abbie's rosy cheek.

"Really? This is not just post-orgasm garbage, is it?"

"No, it really isn't. It all makes sense now. I'm falling in love with you," Ren said as she kissed Abbie before she had the chance to gauge her reaction.

Abbie felt her heart jump with joy, a kaleidoscope of butterflies invading her stomach. "Thank goodness for that because I *already* love you," she admitted, holding Ren close.

"Are you sure you're not just saying that because I'm good at massages?" Ren giggled, feeling the same wave of joy.

"Absolutely!"

The pair laughed as they laid together, enjoying the moment. Everything had fallen into place, and Ren finally felt ready to open up her heart again. Abbie finally felt real love. It was nothing like the kind she had felt before. She didn't deny that she had once loved Adam, but it was nothing like this. With Ren, it felt like loving her was the easiest and best thing she had ever experienced. It rolled out of her body like soft words from her tongue.

Nothing had ever made her feel like that.

Nothing, apart from Ren.

EPILOGUE

One Year Later

"Ren has a free slot at five today if that's good for you, Miss Anderson?" Abbie asked as she sat at the reception desk in Ren's clinic.

Things had changed a lot over the past year. Abbie left her boring office job and started working in the clinic, managing Ren's business and helping her out with organizing things. She became a personal assistant, with many added benefits, including free massages, unlimited holiday days, and incredible sex.

"That's great. We'll see you later today

then!" Abbie ended the call and smiled as Ren walked in with two frothy coffees.

"You are excellent at this. I can't believe you work with me now. I absolutely love it!" Ren said, handing over a drink along with a packet of sugar.

"Me too. I feel free. I feel like I've escaped the rat race. We're also making much more money now, and you definitely needed some help organizing things," Abbie giggled.

"Well, I have some exciting news. I'm thinking about building an extension onto the clinic here and employing extra staff. I think this place can really grow," Ren said with optimism, her red hair bouncing over her shoulders.

"Oh my god, Ren! That's so exciting. I can help you do big things here. Together we can make this work," Abbie said as she stood up and kissed Ren gently, touching her soft face with her delicate fingertips.

"Your working hard is helping me out and really paying off. I think I could see a future for us, jetting off into the sunset whenever we wish. I could get this place running itself, allowing me to really cut back on my hours," Ren held Abbie as she fantasized about their future.

"That sounds like a dream," Abbie replied with another soft kiss.

"Fancy dinner out later to celebrate?" Ren asked.

Abbie grabbed her hand and licked her lips, "Absolutely."

∽

AFTER REN HAD FINISHED with her last appointment, she quickly showered and made herself look sexy to take Abbie out on a hot date. They went to their favorite Italian restaurant in town. As they approached the restaurant, Ren seemed quieter than usual.

"Is everything okay? Are you tired? We can quickly eat and leave if you want to sleep," Abbie asked as they made their way toward the front doors.

"I'm completely okay. I think I'm just famished," Ren replied, lacking conviction in her words.

"Okay then!" Abbie smiled as they were asked to wait by the front door.

She couldn't help but notice Ren make

strange eye contact with the man at the front desk.

"What's going on here?" she asked as her brows furrowed together.

"Hello and welcome. Let me show you to your table." The friendly maître d' said with a wide grin and gesturing hand.

"Oh, thank you! What splendid service," Abbie said as she followed him through the restaurant toward an area in the back.

"Just through here, miss," the host said as he gestured toward a private room.

As soon as Abbie walked through, she was in awe of the candle-lit room, a pleasing floral aroma circulating through the air. She turned back to look at Ren in shock, at once noticing that Ren was on one knee behind her, holding a small black box.

"Abbie, I'm not going to mess around anymore. Will you marry me? I love you so much. Every day I wake up next to you is the best day of my life," Ren said as she opened the box to display a beautiful ring with a shining blue stone matching the color of her eyes.

"Oh my god! Yes, yes, yes, a million

times, yes!" Abbie exclaimed as she reached out to hug Ren.

"Fantastic news! Fabulous!" the waiter shouted from the doorway as the other patrons and staff in the restaurant started to applaud their engagement.

Ren couldn't help but smile from ear to ear as she slipped the elegant ring onto Abbie's finger. It glided on with ease and settled itself nicely into place.

"I love it, and I love you. Thank you so much. You're my world," Abbie said with a tear streaming down her face.

"God, I was so nervous!" Ren laughed as the red in her cheeks began to fade.

"We are still eating, right?" Abbie giggled.

"Absolutely! I'm having a beautiful dinner with my perfect fiancé," Ren said as she leaned in and kissed Abbie softly in the dimly lit room.

Her heart was so full as she held her love close, knowing she would never let Abbie go.

THE END

THANK YOU FOR READING!

Hey, thank you so much for reading my book. I really do hope that you enjoyed it! I would be grateful if you could spare a moment to leave a review on Amazon – they really do make a difference for Indie authors like myself.

Mailing List

Please sign up to my mailing to be the first to know about my new releases! You'll also receive monthly free stuff as a little thank you:

https://mailchi.mp/2a09276da35f/graceparkeswrites

Social Media

If you'd like to get in touch or keep up to date with what I'm up to, here's where to find me!

Twitter:
    https://www.twitter.com/GraceParkesFic

Facebook:
    https://www.facebook.com/graceparkesauthor

Email:
    graceparkeswrites@hotmail.com

Instagram: @graceparkeswrites

TikTok: @graceparkesauthor

Facebook Group

I have a readers group on Facebook that I share new information with about my latest work in progress! It's good fun. If you search **Grace Parkes Lesfic Group** on Facebook, you can join in the fun!

Please check out my other books. They are all available to read for free on Kindle Unlimited.

Code of Conduct

Chief Psychiatric Nurse, Victoria, is blown away and intrigued by her new student nurse, Ella. Can Victoria maintain her professionalism when faced with temptation? Can Ella refrain from crossing the line?

Victoria is used to being in charge, but her own values are pushed when she has to mentor her new and eager student nurse, Ella.

Passion takes her by surprise, putting her career on the line.

Will Victoria adhere to The Code of Conduct or risk it all for Ella?

Get it here: getbook.at/codeofconduct

The Business of Pleasure

The Iconic and influential Zora Drake, has spent her entire life working hard to be successful. With an empire to run, Zora struggles to find time for women, until she discovers the unusual services offered by young glamorous Isabella.

Zora is an icon in the vibrant city of Aperth. Her guarded heart and busy lifestyle leave her with no time to think about any romantic involvement with women. Intrigued by the services offered by glamorous city girl Isabella, Zora is keen to know more. Life changes quickly is this hearty romance.

Rivalry in the city puts Zora's safety at risk, will fear force her to confront what is important to her?

Can Isabella break into Zora's frosty heart, or is there too much on the line including Isabella's safety?

Get it here: https://getbook.at/thebusinessofpleasure

Before Her

Cara Taylor has spent her life in a small village without much excitement. She works in a bar, lives with her best friend and without realising is in need of something new and exciting.

After meeting her best friend's new tenant Frankie, she is desperate to find out more.

Can Cara break down Frankie's barriers and find love in the land that time forgot?

Get it here: getbook.at/BeforeHer

Please Mistress

Fiona can't wait to leave her dysfunctional family life, her safe boyfriend and the small town she grew up in far behind her when she goes to Music School in the city.

She needs to figure out what she wants in life and love, but there seem to be more questions than answers.

Then there is her growing obsession with her aloof singing teacher, Joss Red.

Will Fiona find a way to tell Joss about her fantasies?

Get it here: getbook.at/pleasemistress

Bittersweet She

Tasha Robinson thought her average life would never change. For years Tasha had continued to stay in the same job, town and stale relationship – none of which brought excitement into her life.

As societal pressures smother Tasha, a weekend away with her best friend changes everything, but has it changed for the better?

Tasha meets a captivating girl who takes her breath away and is forced to make some difficult decisions which could potentially change her life forever.

getbook.at/BittersweetShe

Her Secret

Sarah and Emily had everything they ever wanted, except a happy relationship.

After new girl Megan Jenkinson started working alongside Sarah, life began to change.

They embark on a heated affair which takes them both by surprise, especially Megan who had always been into guys.

Lies and deceit take everyone on a gripping adventure throughout this new steamy lesfic by exciting author Grace Parkes.

Disclaimer - this book contains cheating please don't read if you do not like this topic

Get it here: mybook.to/hersecretlesfic

Guitar Girl

Ava Sierra knew from a young age that she was destined for the stage. What she didn't know was the turbulent drama that was on its way into her life.

As she battles it out for the chance to break through into the music industry with her rebellious band, she collides with rival Charlotte Thunder who seems all too familiar.

Loud music, unrequited love and an unexpected chain of events will keep you turning pages in this new exciting lesfic by budding author Grace Parkes.

Get it here: getbook.at/GuitarGirl

Lost in Desire

Naomi Lawson is straight. She runs her own cleaning company and is determined to make it successful.

Her new client intrigues her like no-one ever has- and this client is a woman.

Naomi begins to wonder what it would be like to be with another woman and this woman is so tempting yet so emotionally unavailable?

Get it here: https://getbook.at/lostindesire

Once Again – Thank you!
Grace x

Printed in Dunstable, United Kingdom